My Father Doesn't Know
About the Woods and Me

To Sara and Amy
— D. H.

To Sam's wilderness spirit
— M. H.

My Father Doesn't Know About the Woods and Me

by Dennis Haseley

Illustrated by Michael Hays

ATHENEUM   1988   NEW YORK

When my father calls me, I'm trying to paint a picture of a deer.

"Let's take our walk now," he says, and I'm already out the door. Ahead of us, yellow leaves are turning in the sunlight like fire.

"Let's run down this hill," I say, and he smiles and says, "No, you go on."

So I run down. And I wish he was running with me, because then he'd know. About the woods and me.

He'd know that past the second tree—the one that's a little scary because it has a face in its bark—I leap over a log. And I fall to all fours, but not like a baby, no! Stronger and quick. My eyes turn yellow. I feel the muscles in my arms and legs coil like springs. I feel pads growing on my hands and feet as I run through the trees. Nothing can catch me, and the leaves speed by beneath me *red brown gold red brown gold*. My lungs burn as I burst to the top of a hill and give a howl.

It crashes into the pale moon like it's hitting a frying pan.
Then I tear back through the woods, and on the trail
next to me, through the trees, like seeing someone
through the spaces in a picket fence, I see my father.
He's just walking and whistling, as if everything's the
same, and I break from the woods in front of him and
disappear again in the trees on the other side of the trail.
He doesn't know that the wolf he sees is me.

Pretty soon I'm back by his side again.

"Have a good run?" he asks.

I nod, and then I give a grin that shows all my teeth.
There are teeth on the ferns by the trail.

We come to the big gray rock where my father likes to stop and catch his breath. The woods are thicker here. My father doesn't know what can happen here. When he stretches and yawns, I just have to run from him and spread my arms! I pump my arms up and down and up and down. It's hard work, but pretty soon I'm rising through the trees. Branches flick my cheeks, leaves pop, and then...

I'm way above the trees that look like broccoli below. I open my arms as wide as they'll go, and up in the sky it's like I'm floating in water, with the sun on my back and the wind rippling over me. My eyes are so sharp I can see everything. I can see the point of red on my paint-brush. I can see the rabbits with their worried noses. I can see the mice scurrying for cover, chanting *hawk, hawk.* And standing now, by the big gray rock, I can see my father. He looks up, shades his eyes with his hand. I wish he knew that flash of wings was me.

After lunch, we walk toward a stream. He says he'll fish a little, and I can have a turn. But you have to stay so still to fish, and I can feel the current building in my arms and legs. I start to walk away, from rock to rock with my arms out, while the stream beneath me rushes faster.

"I'll be here," he calls after me, and I wave to show him I've heard.

Around a bend in the stream, my foot slips, but that's fine, so I slide into the water, feel my skin turn smooth and silver, feel my feet melt together into a tail. I'm diving deep into that cold water, so fast, and with just a nod of my head, I can dodge logs with bark coming off and jagged black rocks.

I zip downstream, and I see his fishing line in the water, a little shiny hook at the end. The water's so fast that in a second I'm past it. Then ten feet downstream I leap! The sun catches my side. Drops fall off me like bits of rainbow, and I flick my tail like a silver light, trying to catch my father's eyes. He doesn't know that I'm the one that gets away.

Further down, I flip onto shore, and pretty soon I'm dry again. I run back up the rocks in the stream. But my father's not where I thought he'd be. I figure he's up the trail, so I cross the stream and run that way. But I don't see him. The sun's coming through the woods in big slanting beams, and underneath the trees, darkness is growing in patches like moss. I feel tears in my cheeks, way down behind my eyes. I run up the trail, searching.

When I turn a bend, I come upon the deer.

He's twice as tall as me, and his antlers sweep up from his head like wings, and end in points like stars. On his coat, the shadows of the leaves look like mountains, the shadows of the branches like rivers, and as they move on his coat in the wind, it's like he's traveling even though he's standing still.

As I stare at him in the slanting light, he starts moving his head, driving his antlers into one tree, and another. He cuts into dead branches, knocks out hunks of bark that fall at my feet, and chips spray my face like rain. The trees are shaking as if in a huge wind, and I start to back away, but in all that sound he hears me move, and turns his head toward me. The trees grow still.

I stand there, afraid to step, and he looks into my eyes for a long time in the silence, a leaf still swinging from his antlers. I see the trees rise up and up behind him, and I feel so small, but safe with him, too.

He shakes his head once, and again. Then he turns and steps from the trail into the forest, and I see the muscles working above his legs, moving along his neck. As he disappears into the woods, his antlers hook the branches so high above his head, and leave them swaying.

My heart's pounding as I run down the trail, around the bend, back to the stream. Everything is so quiet it's like I'm running through a painting. My father's just stepping out of the woods. I don't call out yet, but just watch him. His strides seem strong and smooth.

Now he turns and looks down into my eyes, and it's a look I know, old and deep as the woods. He leans down and lifts me up in his arms. Behind him now, I can see that where he's come through the trees, something has hooked the high branches, and left them swaying.

Text copyright © 1988 by Dennis Haseley
Illustrations copyright © 1988 by Michael Hays

Atheneum
Macmillan Publishing Company
866 Third Avenue, New York, NY 10022
Collier Macmillan Canada, Inc.

Composition by Linoprint Composition Co., Inc., New York, New York
Printed and bound by Toppan Printing Company in Japan

First Edition

10   9   8   7   6   5   4   3   2   1

Library of Congress Cataloging-in-Publication Data

Haseley, Dennis.
My father doesn't know about the woods and me/by Dennis Haseley;
illustrated by Michael Hays.—1st ed.   p.   cm.
Summary: As a child walks in the woods with his father, he seems
to become other animals enjoying the freedom of nature.
ISBN 0-689-31365-9
[1. Fathers and sons—Fiction.   2. Imagination—Fiction.
3. Forests and forestry—Fiction.]   I. Hays, Michael, 1956–   ill.
II. Title.
PZ7.H2688My   1988
[E]—dc19
87–30295   CIP   AC